OUT OF THIS WORLD

D1508852

Based on the major motion picture

Adapted by Sarah Nathan

Based on the Screenplay Written by Matt Lopez and Mark Bomback and Andy Fickman

Based on Characters Created by Alexander Key

Executive Producers Mario Iscovich, Ann Marie Sanderlin

Produced by Andrew Gunn

Directed by Andy Fickman

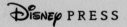

New York

All rights reserved. Published by Disney Press, an imprint of Disney Book Group.
No part of this book may be reproduced or transmitted in any form or by any means,
electronic or mechanical, including photocopying, recording, or by any information storage
and retrieval system, without written permission from the publisher. For information
address Disney Press, 114 Fifth Avenue, New York, New York 10011-5690.
Printed in the United States of America
First Edition
1 3 5 7 9 10 8 6 4 2
Library of Congress Catalog Card Number on file.
ISBN 978-1-4231-1988-3
Visit disneybooks.com

Chapter 1

One dark night over the Nevada desert, a small spaceship sped toward Earth.

On board the ship were a brother and sister, Seth and Sara.

Unfortunately, their arrival was noticed
by people at a nearby military base. They
ordered Henry Burke, an expert on alien
life, to go to the site where the spaceship
had landed.

Burke ordered his men to search the desert. They looked for any sign of aliens.

But Seth and Sara were able to get away.

They were on a special mission: to save
their home planet and protect Earth.
They headed for Las Vegas.

Sara and Seth knew they were going to need money. In the city, they stopped at a bank machine. Without touching the buttons, they withdrew money. Next, they needed a ride.

Chapter 2

Jack Bruno was a cabdriver. He didn't
like trouble. But this particular night,
there was an outer-space convention
going on. Jack sighed. A quiet night was
out of the question.

After taking a quick break, Jack found Sara and Seth in his cab.

"We require your transportation services immediately," Seth told Jack.

Jack saw that the boy was holding a high-tech gadget.

Seth didn't tell Jack that it was a special compass. He just told him to go to the desert. Just then, three black cars came racing down the highway. It was Henry Burke! He was hot on Seth and Sara's trail!

What Jack didn't know was Seth and Sara had special powers!

They used their powers to make Henry Burke's car crash into Jack's cab.

Jack was angry! He got out of the cab and warned Burke to stop following them. Burke let Jack and his two young passengers go.

Chapter 3

Jack got back in his cab and they continued down the highway. Sara and Seth sat quietly in the back. The road became a dirt path. The path ended in front of an old, empty cabin.

"We're here," Seth said.

Seth gave Jack the large pile of cash from his pocket to pay for the ride. Then he and Sara rushed out of the taxi and into the cabin. Jack counted the money. The kids had overpaid him. He got out of his car and headed after them.

CRASH! A loud noise came from inside. Jack walked slowly toward the door. Some of the windows were boarded up and others were smashed. Jack held a piece of wood in his hand for protection.

Inside, Jack found Sara and Seth hiding under a sofa. Seth covered Jack's mouth, signaling him not to speak. Someone bad was in the room!

Seth took out his high-tech compass and tried to get a reading. Sara looked at Jack, concern in her eyes.

"You should not have risked your life by following us," she said.

Now Jack was really confused. What kind of trouble were these kids in?

Seth placed the compass on a wall
behind an old refrigerator. The gadget-
glowed and spun around. Then the wall
moved, revealing an old stone staircase!

Chapter 4

Seth and Sara climbed down the steps.
Jack watched them disappear and sighed.
It looked like he was going, too.

The stairway led to a huge underground
garden filled with every kind of plant
and tree imaginable.

They thought they heard a sound coming from deep in the garden. Seth and Sara were worried they were being followed.

Growing from the ground were large balloonlike bags filled with swirling gases. Jack tried to touch one of the bags, but they were covered with goo!

As Sara and Seth slowly moved though the garden, their eyes were focused on their compass. Sara took a pendant from the necklace she wore and slid it inside the orb. Something popped out.

"What is that thing?" Jack asked.

"It is what we came for," Sara told him.

Suddenly, there were mini-explosions all around them—caused by a masked intruder! Jack knocked him down. Then the three escaped up the stairs and raced out the cabin door. They dove into the taxi, and Jack sped away.

Sara used her powers to push Jack's foot, making the gas pedal go all the way to the floor. The taxi raced down the highway.

"We can't let him destroy it, Sara,"
Seth said, looking at the object clutched
in her hand.

Chapter 5

Sara and Seth told Jack who the intruder was. It was a Siphon. The Siphon was an alien. Its mission was to destroy them. It wanted the device they were holding. Sara and Seth explained that they were from outer space. And they needed Jack's help.

Jack was confused, and his taxi was a mess. He found a small auto-repair shop to fix it. They headed into the town for food, and Sara and Seth explained that their planet was dying.

Their parents were scientists, and the
object they had pulled from the orb
was filled with their parents' research.
If Seth and Sara didn't bring it back to
their planet, their leaders would take
over Earth!

They didn't realize Henry Burke had tracked them down.

Burke tried to capture them while they were eating.

Seth, Sara, and Jack snuck out of the diner before Burke and his men could see them. They had to get back to their car and get out of town.

They ended up in a junkyard where a dog was standing guard. Sara used her powers to make friends with the dog and Jack raced to get his car.

Sara and Seth urged Jack to take them to their spaceship. When Jack didn't reply, Seth looked over at his sister. "We only have each other. No one's going to help us, no human, especially not this human."

But Seth was wrong. Jack had an idea. He knew someone who could help them. Turning the cab back toward Las Vegas, Jack took a deep breath. His planet was about to be destroyed. Aliens existed. And he had two teenagers who could save everyone. Jack's adventure had only just begun.